Guinea Pigs
Far and Near
by Kate Duke

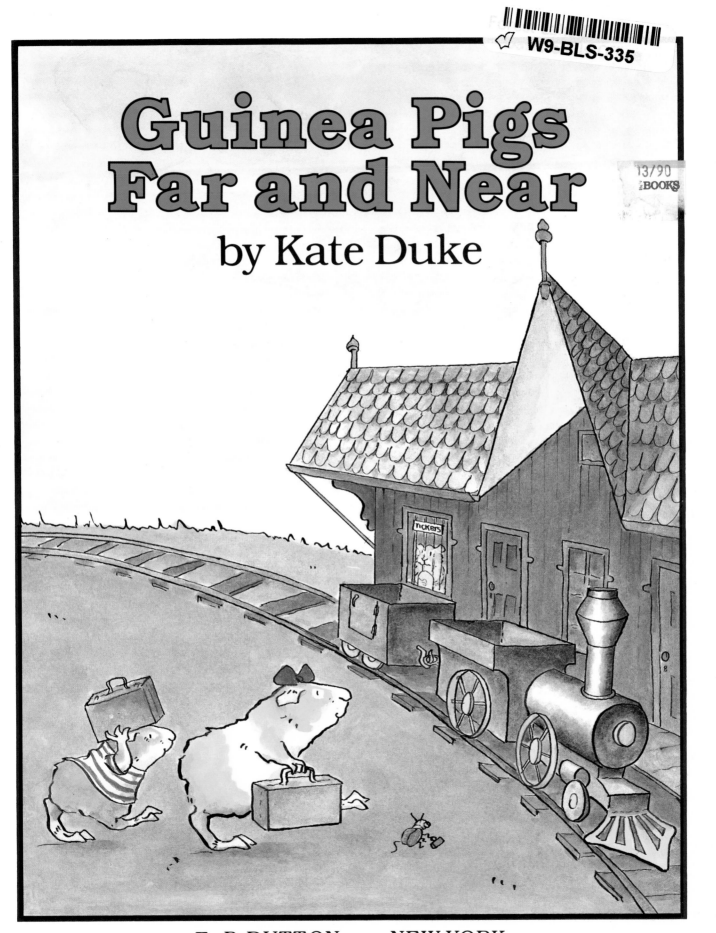

E. P. DUTTON · NEW YORK

Library of Congress number 84-1580
ISBN 0-525-44480-7

Published in the United States by
E. P. Dutton, New York, N.Y.,
a division of NAL Penguin Inc.

Published simultaneously in Canada by
Fitzhenry & Whiteside Limited, Toronto

Editor: Ann Durell   Designer: Riki Levinson

Printed in Hong Kong by South China Printing Co.
First Unicorn Edition 1989
10 9 8 7 6 5 4 3 2 1

to friends and family near and far

Apart

Far

Near

Together

Over

Under

Around

Through

Up   High

Above

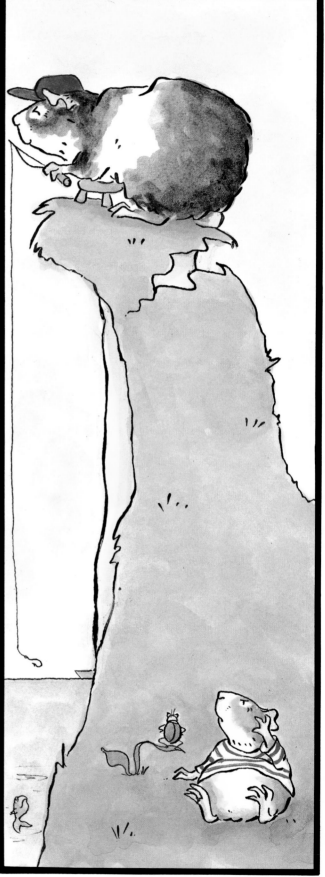

Down   Low

Below

Inside out

Upside down

Right side up

Right side out

Ahead

Across

Aboard

Away

Where?

There

Nowhere

Here!

First

Next

Last

Behind

Beside

Between

Among